ALIENS IN MY NEST

Squib Meets The Teen Creature

Written and Illustrated by Larry Shles

JALMAR PRESS 1988

Library of Congress Cataloging-in-Publication Data

Shles, Larry.
Aliens in my Nest

Summary: Squib comes home from summer camp
to find that his older brother, Andrew,
has turned into a snarly, surly,
defiant, and non-communicative adolescent.
Aliens explores the effect of Andrew's
new behavior on Squib and
the entire family unit.

[1. Fables.   2. Owls — Fiction.   3. Self-esteem — Adolescence Fiction]
I. Title.   II. Title: Aliens in my Nest
Library of Congress Catalog Card Number: 88-80770
ISBN 0-915190-49-4

Printed in the United States of America

Cloth   P   Pbk.   AL   10 9 8 7 6 5 4 3 2

Dedicated to all the families
that have experienced the
wonders of 'owldolescence'.

ALIENS IN MY NEST

Squib Meets The Teen Creature

Summer camp was dragging to a close. "I can't wait to get back home," Squib thought. "Mom's going to love the God's eye I made for her. And wait until Andrew sees how great I'm doing at basketball."

Andrew was Squib's older brother. He was a source of great joy and pride to the whole family.

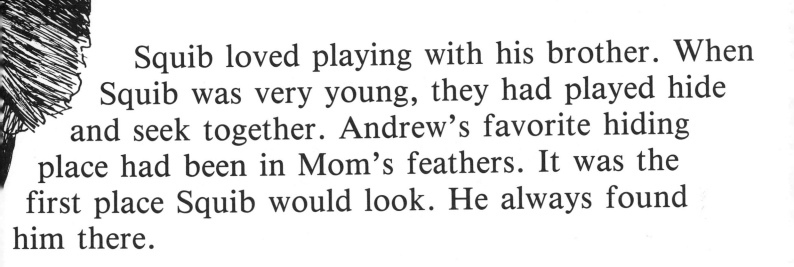

Squib loved playing with his brother. When Squib was very young, they had played hide and seek together. Andrew's favorite hiding place had been in Mom's feathers. It was the first place Squib would look. He always found him there.

As Squib got older, Andrew began coaching him in sports.

Squib often shared his dreams of the future with his brother.

"When I become a star, will you come to see my games, Andrew?" he asked.

"I wouldn't miss a one!" Andrew would cheer. "I believe in you, Squib! I'll practice with you until you become a star!"

"What a great friend my brother is!" Squib thought.

"What's going on around here?" Squib wondered as he arrived home from camp. The ground was covered with strange nuts and knots. "I don't remember seeing these before," he thought.

Then Squib heard a peculiar chanting. He looked up. He couldn't believe his eyes. What had happened to Andrew?!

"I **am** who I **am**! Who **am** I? Who **am** I?" Andrew was chanting over and over again.

Squib moved closer. "Hi, Andrew. I'm back. Let's play some ball!"

"Beat it, punk," snarled Andrew. "I don't play with children anymore."

"But Andrew...."

"You heard what I said!"

Andrew's surliness shocked Squib. He went hunting for Mom and Dad. They would know what was wrong with Andrew.

Squib found Dad staring into space. He looked totally nuts.

"I'll show **him** who's boss! **Who's** boss? **Who's** boss?" Dad was chanting over and over again.

"Hi, Dad. I'm back. I want to play with Andrew and he's being mean to me."

"Uh, huh," mumbled Dad, and he resumed his chanting.

Dad seemed to be on another planet. Squib went in search of Mom.

He found Mom staring at a wall. She was tied up in knots.

"I did **all** I could! **All** I could? **All** I could?" Mom was chanting, over and over again.

"Hi, Mom. I'm back. Look at the God's eye I made for you."

"Uh, huh," mumbled Mom, and she resumed her chanting.

Mom seemed to be on another planet, too.

Squib went to bed alone that night to the strange chanting of his family. They seemed to have gone crazy.

In the morning Squib rushed to Andrew's room, eager to see if he was ready to play. An awesome barricade now surrounded Andrew's side of the nest.

"Andrew! Oh, Andrew!" Squib called through the fence.

"You can't come in, kid!" snarled Andrew. "I'm getting ready to go out with my friends. You wait out there."

Squib waited for what seemed like forever.

Suddenly Andrew appeared. Or **was** it Andrew? Perhaps the real Andrew had been kidnapped by invaders from another world. This could be one of the alien creatures masquerading as his brother. Maybe Andrew was **from** another planet.

"I guess you don't want to shoot some baskets now?" asked Squib, softly.

"You've got that right!" grunted Andrew. "I don't even want to be seen with you."

"I **am** who I **am**! Who **am** I? Who **am** I?" Andrew sang while he plunked on his guitar.

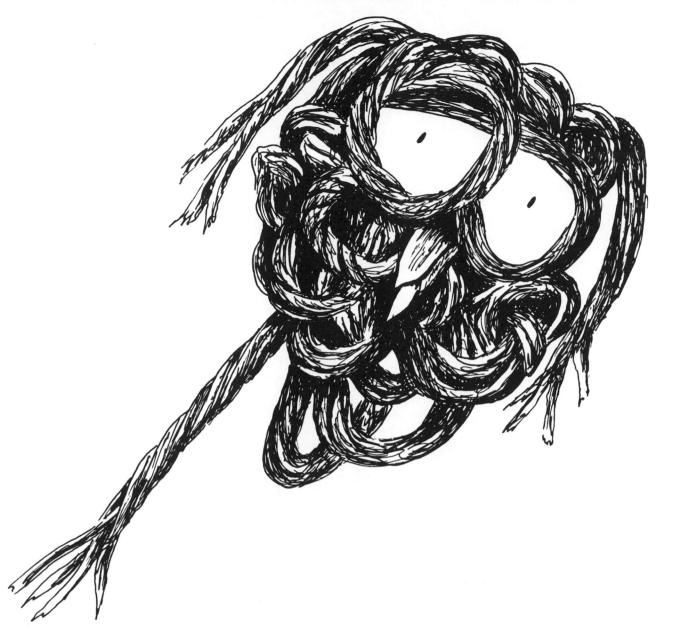

When Mom and
Dad saw Andrew looking
like an alien from another world, they lost
control. Dad became seriously unbalanced.
Mom careened off the walls.

"You are not leaving the nest looking like
that!" bellowed Dad.

"Is this how I raised him?" babbled Mom.

"You can't tell me how to look!" snarled
Andrew.

"That's what you think," screamed Mom.
"Go to your room and smooth out your
feathers this instant!"

"No!" yelled Andrew.

"Yes!" shrieked Mom.

"NO!" yelled Andrew.

"YES!" shrieked Mom.

"NO!" "YES!" "NO!" "YES!"
"I hate you!" exploded Andrew.

All shell broke loose. Squib hid. "This family **has** gone crazy," he thought.

Squib was desperate to get through to his brother. The next morning he tried a new approach.

"Squib calling Andrew! Are you in there?"

"Huh?"

"Have you changed your mind about playing ball?" Squib tooted.

"Leave me alone."

"I don't understand what's wrong with you," pleaded Squib.

"They're the ones
who are wrong,"
snapped Andrew.
   "Who?"
   "Mom and Dad,"
Andrew hissed
with disgust.
   "Mom and Dad?"
   "Yeah! They're always
getting on my nerves.
It's those dumb
feathers of theirs.
I feel like a
caged animal."

"I'm tired of all their stupid rules," Andrew exclaimed. "I want to be free!"

ALGONKIAN ELEMENTARY

"Mom and Dad expect me to be perfect. One minute they want me to be the adorable little angel I used to be. The next minute they want me to be like some perfect adult. Well, I'm not a child anymore. And I'm not an adult. I **am** who I **am**! Who **am** I? Who **am** I?"

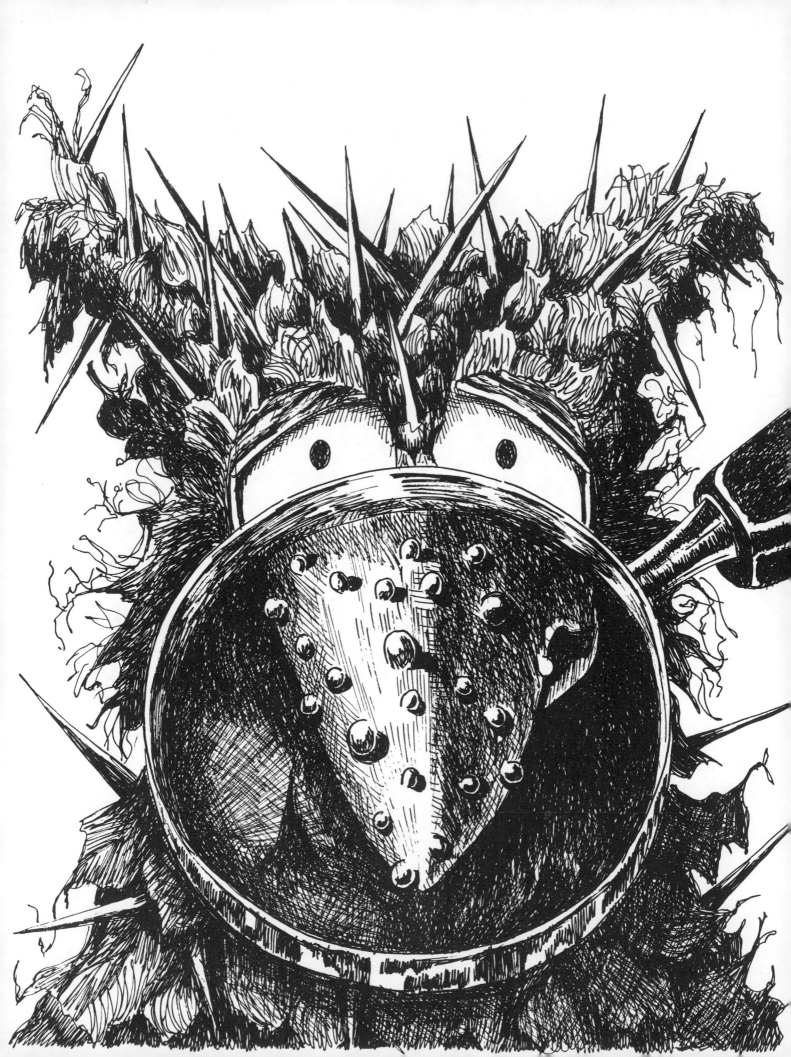

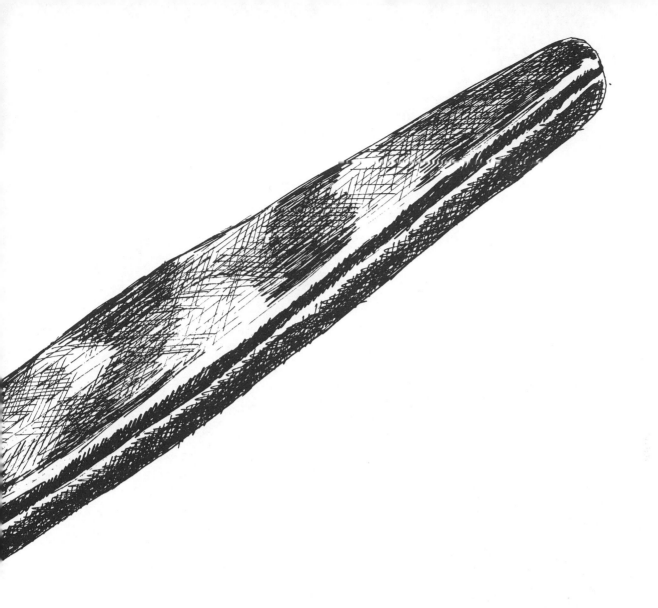

"One thing's for sure," moaned Andrew. "I am not a perfect anything. Look at the bumps on my beak. And my beady eyes. And have you ever seen such clumpy feathers and stumpy tufts?"

"I am who I am. Bumpy, beady, clumpy, stumpy," Andrew chanted.

"There is one thing that is perfect about me, however — —

my room!
I decorated it.
Do *you* see
anything wrong
with it?"

"And what's wrong with the food I eat? Do Mom and Dad really expect me to eat butterfly wing casseroles and daddy-long-leg drumsticks? Real owls don't eat that junk. I'll take some pasta con crawlers and spicy swamp sauce any day."

"Some of the essential food groups are missing from this mess," Squib thought to himself.

A loud screech and raucous hooting interrupted the discussion.

"This conversation is ended," Andrew snapped suddenly. "My friends are waiting for me. Aren't they great?! They're the only ones who understand me."

"I can be who I am with my friends. I don't need Mom and Dad. I don't need any of their rules. I hate their stupid rules."

"I'm getting out of here now," Andrew hooted coldly. "This family is dull and you are the dullest, Squib."

"But I'm your brother," tooted Squib.
"Will we ever be able to play again?"

Andrew didn't answer.
He was with his friends now.

As time passed, things got worse in the nest. Andrew grew to a huge size. At the same time, Mom and Dad seemed to shrink.

Often Andrew would amuse himself by toying with his parents.

And when he tired of that game, he would make up another one. Squib despaired. How he wanted the old Andrew back. Mom and Dad did more than despair.

Mom had reached the end of her rope. Dad had cracked up. Quivering and jibbering, they took Andrew to the doctor.

"This family is a disaster," announced the doctor.

"It's Andrew," mumbled Mom. "I fear he is unbalanced."

"He is," agreed the doctor. "Actually, you all are."

Mom and Dad gasped.

"Don't worry, though," continued the doctor. "It's a common condition. Your family is suffering from 'owldolescence'. It is a time when the brain goes to sleep and things get totally out of gland."

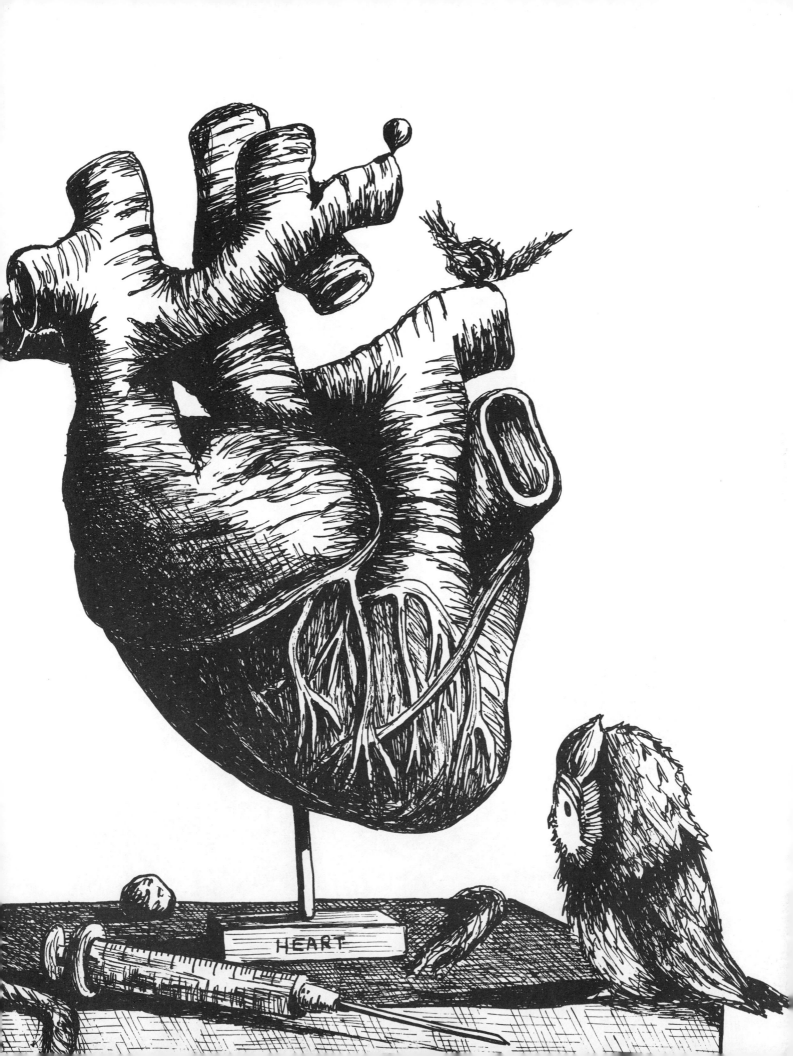

PATIENCE
RESPECT
COMMUNICATION
UNDERSTANDING
DIAL 911

"What can be done to fix Andrew?" asked Dad.

"Do we have to get a shot?" tooted Squib.

The doctor smiled. "Here are a few rules to remember when your family is suffering from 'owldolescence'. Plant them firmly in your minds and practice them daily."

Squib was as confused as ever. The words on the chart just weren't sinking in.

"But when will Andrew be ready to play with me again?" Squib implored.

The doctor nodded gently. "Just be patient. This is only a stage that Andrew is going through."

"I guess I must have stage fright," thought Mom.

"It is all part of the *natural order* of things," continued the doctor.

"Is it too late to cancel *this order*?" Dad wondered.

"Patience, Respect, Communication, Understanding," the doctor chanted over and over again.

The family returned home with the words planted firmly in their minds.

Things were better for a few minutes. Then everyones' brains went to sleep again and they forgot the words. There was another terrible blow-up.

"I can't stand it anymore!" screamed Andrew. "I'm leaving this place!"

"I guess I showed **him** who's boss," hooted Dad.

"If you must leave, please be careful," cried Mom.

"Will you ever come back and play with me?" pleaded Squib . It was then that Squib noticed a crack in Andrew's giant body.

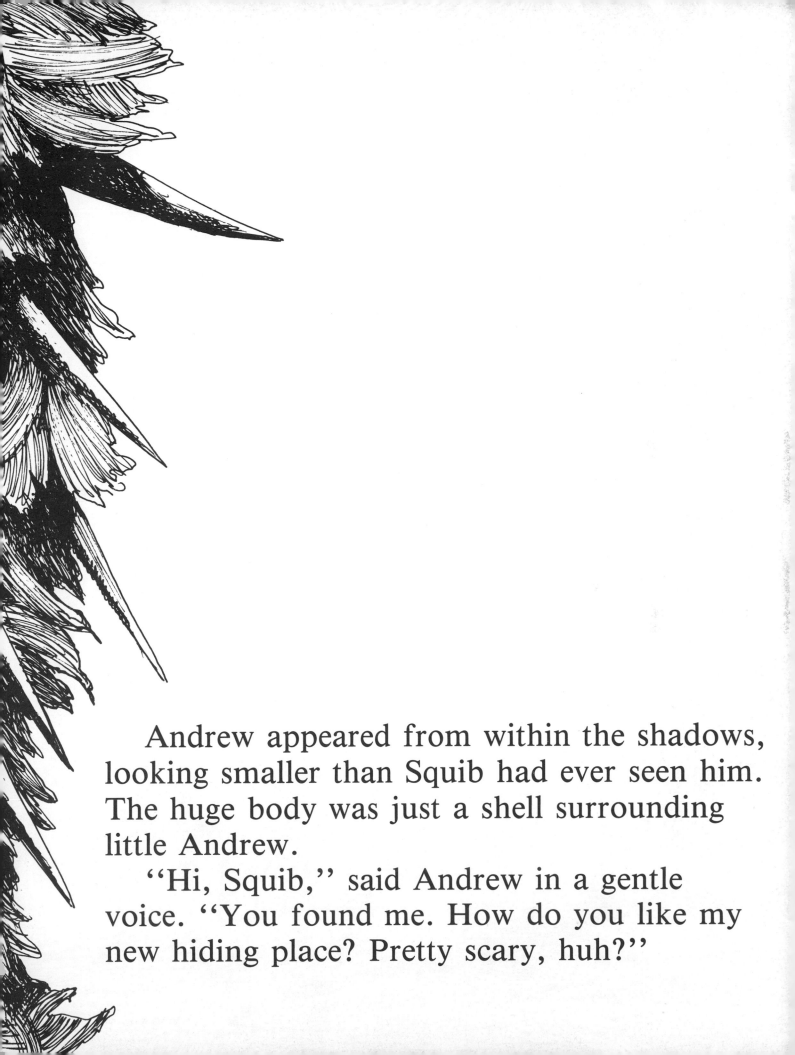

Andrew appeared from within the shadows, looking smaller than Squib had ever seen him. The huge body was just a shell surrounding little Andrew.

"Hi, Squib," said Andrew in a gentle voice. "You found me. How do you like my new hiding place? Pretty scary, huh?"

Then a ball rolled out from the crack and stopped at Squib's feet.

"Hold on to this while I'm gone, Squib. This is a journey I have to make alone. Practice up! We'll play when I get back."

"And one more thing," whispered Andrew, "Tell Mom and Dad that I love them very much."

Then the crack closed up. The giant shell swaggered a few steps and lifted off toward the sky.

With Andrew gone, the family slowly returned to normal. One day Squib found his mother staring at the sky and crying.

Squib patted her gently. "Mom, you and I can play. I will never act like Andrew. I will never leave you. I promise."

Mom looked down at the tiny thorns beginning to appear on Squib. For just a moment she smiled.

"I know, Squib. I know."

Learning The Skills of Peacemaking
An Activity Guide for Elementary-Age Children

"Global peace begins with you. Guide develops this fundamental concept in fifty lessons. If this curriculum was a required course in every elementary school in every country, we would see world peace in our children's lifetimes." — *Letty Cottin Pogrebin*, Ms. Magazine
0-915190-46-X $21.95
8½ × 11   paperback, illus.

Project Self-Esteem EXPANDED
A Parent Involvement Program for Elementary-Age Children

An innovative parent-support program that promotes children's self-worth. "Project Self Esteem is the most extensively tested and affordable drug and alcohol preventative program available."

0-915190-59-1   **$39.95**
8½ × 11   paperback, illus.

The Two Minute Lover
Announcing A New Idea In Loving Relationships

No one is foolish enough to imagine that s/he *automatically* deserves success. Yet, almost everyone thinks that they automatically deserve sudden and continuous success in marriage. Here's a book that helps make that belief a reality.
0-915190-52-4 $9.95
6 × 9   paperback, illus.

Reading, Writing and Rage

An autopsy of one profound school failure, disclosing the complex processes behind it and the secret rage that grew out of it.

Must reading for anyone working with learning disabled, functional illiterates, or juvenile delinquents.

0-915190-42-7 $16.95
5½ × 8½   paperback

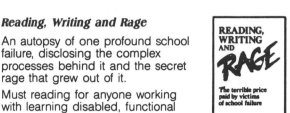

Feel Better Now
30 Ways to Handle Frustrations in Three Minutes or Less

A practical menu of instant stress reduction techniques, designed to be used right in the middle of high-pressure situations. Feel Better Now includes stress management tools for every problem and every personality style.
0-915190-66-4 $9.95
6 × 9 paperback, appendix, biblio.

Esteem Builders

You CAN improve your students' behavior and achievement through building self-esteem. Here is a book packed with classroom- proven techniques, activities, and ideas you can immediately use in your own program or at home.

Ideas, ideas, ideas, for grades K-8 and parents.

0-915190-53-2 $39.95
8½ × 11   paperback, illus.

Good Morning Class—I Love You!
Thoughts and Questions About Teaching from the Heart

A book that helps create the possibility of having schools be places where students, teachers and principals get what every human being wants and needs—LOVE!

0-915190-58-3 $6.95
5½ × 8½ paperback, illus.

I am a blade of grass
A Breakthrough in Learning and Self-Esteem

Help your students become "lifetime learners," empowered with the confidence to make a positive difference in their world (without abandoning discipline or sacrificing essential skill and content acquisition).
0-915190-54-0 $14.95
6 × 9   paperback, illus.

Unlocking Doors to Self-Esteem

Presents innovative ideas to make the secondary classroom a more positive learning experience—socially and emotionally—for students and teachers. Over 100 lesson plans included. Designed for easy infusion into curriculum. Gr. 7-12

0-915190-60-5 $16.95
6 × 9 paperback, illus

SAGE: *Self-Awareness Growth Experiences*

A veritable treasure trove of activities and strategies promoting positive behavior and meeting the personal/social needs of young people in grades 7-12. Organized around affective learning goals and objectives. Over 150 activities.
0-915190-61-3   **$16.95**
6 × 9 paperback, illus.

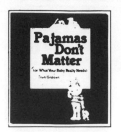

Pajamas Don't Matter:
(or What Your Baby Really Needs)

Here's help for new parents every-
where! Provides valuable information
and needed reassurances to new
parents as they struggle through the
frantic, but rewarding, first years of
their child's life.
0-915190-21-4 $5.95
8½ × 11   paperback, full color

Why Does Santa Celebrate Christmas?

What do wisemen, shepherds and
angels have to do with Santa,
reindeer and elves? Explore this
Christmas fantasy which ties all of
the traditions of Christmas into one
lovely poem for children of all
ages.
0-915190-67-2 $12.95
8 1/2 x 11 hardcover, full color

Feelings Alphabet

Brand-new kind of alphabet book full
of photos and word graphics that will
delight readers of all ages.". . .lively,
candid. . .the 26 words of
this pleasant book express
experiences common to all children."
Library Journal
0-935266-15-1 $7.95
6 × 9   paperback, B/W photos

The Parent Book

A functional and sensitive guide for
parents who want to enjoy every minute of their child's growing years.
Shows how to live with children in
ways that encourage healthy emo-
tional development. Ages 3-14.
0-915190-15-X $9.95
8½ × 11   paperback, illus.

Aliens In My Nest
SQUIB Meets The Teen Creature

Squib comes home from summer
camp to find that his older brother,
Andrew, has turned into a snarly,
surly, defiant, and non-communicative adolescent. *Aliens* explores the
effect of Andrew's new behavior on
Squib and the entire family unit.
0-915190-49-4 $7.95
8½ × 11   paperback, illus.

Hugs & Shrugs
The Continuing Saga of SQUIB

Squib feels incomplete. He has lost a
piece of himself. He searches every
where only to discover that his missing piece has fallen in and not out.
He becomes complete again once
he discovers his own inner-peace.

0-915190-47-8 $7.95
8½ × 11   paperback, illus.

Moths & Mothers/ Feather & Fathers
A Story About a Tiny Owl Named SQUIB

Squib is a tiny owl who cannot fly.
Neither can he understand his feelings. He must face the frustration,
grief, fear, guilt and loneliness that
we all must face at different times in
our lives. Struggling with these feelings, he searches, at least, for
understanding.

0-915190-57-5 $7.95
8½ × 11   paperback, illus.

Hoots & Toots & Hairy Brutes
The Continuing Adventures of SQUIB

Squib—who can only toot—sets out
to learn how to give a mighty hoot.
His attempts result in abject failure.
Every reader who has struggled with
life's limitations will recognize their
own struggles and triumphs in the
microcosm of Squib's forest world. A
parable for all ages from 8 to 80.

0-915190-56-7 $7.95
8½ × 11   paperback, illus.

Do I Have To Go To School Today?
Squib Measures Up!

Squib dreads the daily task of going
to school. In this volume, he
daydreams about all the reasons he
has not to go. But, in the end, Squib
convinces himself to go to school
because his teacher accepts him
"Just as he is!"

0-915190-62-1 $7.95
8½ × 11   paperback, illus.

The Turbulent Teens
Understanding Helping Surviving

"This book should be read by every
parent of a teenager in America. . .It
gives a parent the information
needed to understand teenagers and
guide them wisely."—Dr. Fitzhugh
Dodson, author of *How to Parent,
How to Father, and How to Discipline
with Love.*
0-913091-01-4 $8.95
6 × 9   paperback.

Openmind/Wholemind
Parenting & Teaching Tomorrow's Children Today

A book of powerful possibilities that honors the capacities, capabilities, and potentials of adult and child alike. Uses Modalities, Intelligences, Styles and Creativity to explore how the brain-mind system acquires, processes and expresses experience. Foreword by M. McClaren & C. Charles.
0-915190-45-1 $14.95
7 × 9 paperback
81 B/W photos   29 illus.

Present Yourself! *Captivate Your Audience With Great Presentation Skills*

Become a presenter who is a dynamic part of the message. Learn about Transforming Fear, Knowing Your Audience, Setting The Stage, Making Them Remember and much more. Essential reading for anyone interested in the art of communication. Destined to become the standard work in its field.
0-915190-51-6   paper $9.95
0-915190-50-8   cloth $18.95
6 × 9   paper/cloth. illus.

Unicorns Are Real
A Right-Brained Approach to Learning

Over 100,000 sold. The long-awaited "right hemispheric" teaching strategies developed by popular educational specialist Barbara Vitale are now available. Hemispheric dominance screening instrument included.
0-915190-35-4 $12.95
8½ × 11 paperback, illus.

Unicorns Are Real Poster

Beautifully-illustrated. Guaranteed to capture the fancy of young and old alike. Perfect gift for unicorn lovers, right-brained thinkers and all those who know how to dream. For classroom, office or home display.

JP9027 $4.95
19 × 27   full color

Imagination is the unicorn that lifts us above the mundane chains that bind the minds of many and flies us on fantastic wings to a place where dreams DO come true.

Metaphoric Mind (Revised Ed.)
Here is a plea for a balanced way of thinking and being in a culture that stands on the knife-edge between catastrophe and transformation. The metaphoric mind is asking again, quietly but insistently, for equilibrium. For, after all, equilibrium is the way of nature.
0-915190-68-0 $14.95
7 x 10 paperback, B/W photos

Don't Push Me, I'm Learning as Fast as I Can

Barbara Vitale presents some remarkable insights on the physical growth stages of children and how these stages affect a child's ability, not only to learn, but to function in the classroom.
JP9112 $12.95
Audio Cassette

Tapping Our Untapped Potential

This Barbara Vitale tape gives new insights on how you process information. Will help you develop strategies for improving memory, fighting stress and organizing your personal and professional activities.

JP9111 $12.95
Audio Cassette

Free Flight *Celebrating Your Right Brain*

Journey with Barbara Vitale, from her uncertain childhood perceptions of being "different" to the acceptance and adult celebration of that difference. A book for right-brained people in a left-brained world. Foreword by Bob Samples.
0-915190-44-3 $9.95
5½ × 8½ paperback, illus.

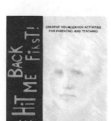

"He Hit Me Back First"
Self-Esteem through Self-Discipline

Simple techniques for guiding children toward self-correcting behavior as they become aware of choice and their own inner authority.
0-915190-36-2 $12.95
8½ × 11 paperback, illus.

Learning To Live, Learning To Love

An inspirational message about the importance of love in everything we do. Beautifully told through words and pictures. Ageless and timeless.
0-915190-38-9 $7.95
6 × 9 paperback, illus.

TA For Tots
(and other prinzes)

Over 500,000 sold.

This innovative book has helped thousands of young children and their parents to better understand and relate to each other. Ages 4-9.
0-915190-12-5 $12.95
8½ × 11   paper, color, illus.

TA For Tots, Vol. II

Explores new ranges of feelings and suggests solutions to problems such as feeling hurt, sad, shy, greedy, or lonely.

Ages 4-9.

0-915190-25-7 $12.95
8½ × 11   paper, color, illus.

TA for Kids
(and grown-ups too)

Over 250,000 sold.

The message of TA is presented in simple, clear terms so youngsters can apply it in their daily lives. Warm Fuzzies abound. Ages 9-13.
0-915190-09-5 $9.95
8½ × 11   paper, color, illus.

TA For Teens
(and other important people)

Over 100,000 sold.

Using the concepts of Transactional Analysis. Dr. Freed explains the ups and downs of adulthood without talking down to teens. Ages 13-18.
0-915190-03-6 $18.95
8½ × 11   paperback, illus.

Original Warm Fuzzy Tale *Learn about "Warm Fuzzies" firsthand.*

Over 100,000 sold.

A classic fairytale . . . with adventure, fantasy, heroes, villains and a moral. Children (and adults, too) will enjoy this beautifully illustrated book.

0-915190-08-7 $7.95
6 × 9   paper, full color, illus.

Songs of The Warm Fuzzy
"All About Your Feelings"

The album includes such songs as Hitting is Harmful, Being Scared, When I'm Angry, Warm Fuzzy Song, Why Don't Parents Say What They Mean, and I'm Not Perfect (Nobody's Perfect).
JP9003 $12.95
                        Cassette

Tot Pac *(Audio-Visual Kit)*

Includes 5 filmstrips, 5 cassettes, 2 record LP album. A *Warm Fuzzy I'm OK* poster, 8 coloring posters, 10 Warm Fuzzies. 1 *TA for Tots* and 92 page *Leader's Manual*. No prior TA training necessary to use Tot Pac in the classroom! Ages 2-9.
JP9032 $150.00
Multimedia program

Kid Pac *(Audio-Visual Kit)*

Teachers, counselors, and parents of pre-teens will value this easy to use program. Each *Kid Pac* contains 13 cassettes, 13 filmstrips, 1 *TA For Kids*, and a comprehensive *Teacher's Guide*, plus 10 Warm Fuzzies. Ages 9-13.
JP9033 $195.00
Multimedia Program

B.L. Winch & Assoc./Jalmar Press
45 Hitching Post Dr., Bldg. 2
Rolling Hills Estates, CA 90274

CALL TOLL FREE: 800/662-9662
In California, Call Collect: 213/547-1240

Please Enclose Check or Credit Card Information

NAME _____

STREET ADDRESS OR R.F.D. _____

CITY/STATE/ZIP _____

☐ Charge to VISA/MC   ☐ Acct. # _____ Exp. Date _____

Cardholder's Signature _____

TITLE	QTY	UNIT PRICE	TOTAL

Sub-Total: _____
CA Sales Tax: _____
Add 10% Shipping/Handling (**Min. $3.00**): _____
TOTAL: _____

Satisfaction guaranteed. Return within 30 days for a full refund. Contact publisher for instructions. Prices subject to change without notice. Foreign checks payable in U.S. dollars.